Tat Rabbit's Treasure

For my Mother and Father

Margaret K. McElderry Books · Macmillan Publishing Company, 866 Third Avenue, New York, NY 10022

Maxwell Macmillan Canada, Inc. · 1200 Eglinton Avenue East, Suite 200, Don Mills, Ontario M3C 3N1

Macmillan Publishing Company is part of the Maxwell Communication Group of Companies.
First edition   Printed in Hong Kong by South China Printing Company (1988) Ltd.   10 9 8 7 6 5 4 3 2 1   The text of this book is set in Berkeley Old Style Medium. The illustrations are rendered in acrylic.

Library of Congress Cataloging-in-Publication Data
Kerins, Anthony.   Tat Rabbit's treasure / written and illustrated by Anthony Kerins.—1st ed.   p.   cm.
Summary: Tat Rabbit and Tig the pig discover an intriguing trunk and wonder what is hidden inside it.
ISBN 0-689-50553-1
[1. Rabbits—Fiction. 2. Pigs—Fiction. 3. Costume—Fiction.]   I. Title.   PZ7.K456Tat 1993   [E]—dc20   92-32600

Anthony Kerins

Tat Rabbit's Treasure

MARGARET K. McELDERRY BOOKS
New York

Maxwell Macmillan Canada
Toronto

Maxwell Macmillan International
New York   Oxford   Singapore   Sydney

Tat Rabbit chuckled.
"A treasure chest!" he cried.

"A box," said Tig.
"A treasure box," Tat insisted.
Tig grinned. "Open it then."

Tat Rabbit stood on tiptoe
and tried to lift the lid.

"Wait!" shouted Tig.
Tat Rabbit jumped.
"What's the matter?" he cried.
"Monsters!" shrieked Tig.
"Where?" asked Tat.

"In the box," said Tig.
"It's probably full of them."

Tat Rabbit gulped.

"But it's not monsters!" he said.
"It's *treasure*! And I'm going to get it!"

This time he stood on Tig's back.
The lid creaked open.
Tat peered in.
"NO. WAIT. STOP!" yelled Tig. "Suppose it's . . ."

But Tat wouldn't listen.
He leaned over the edge of the box.
Suddenly he gave a cry.
His long feet kicked in the air, and in he fell.
"Help! Help! It's dark."
The lid dropped shut.

"Tat!" called Tig. "Tat! Come back. I was only teasing."
But there was no answer.
Tig put his ear against the box.

He could hear grunting and growling sounds.
Tig was frantic.
"Hold on, Tat," he called. "I'll be back in a flash."

Tig came back with a mobile crane.
He opened the lid.

Then he lowered the hook into the box.
"Quick, Tat, grab the rope," he called.

The crane chugged and whirred.
The rope tightened.
Up came the hook.

But Tat wasn't on it.
Instead, there was a horrible monster.
"Oh no! Just like I said," whimpered Tig.
"Wh . . . where's Tat?"
"I've eaten him," growled the monster, "and I'm *still* hungry."

"Yikes! Help!" Tig let go of the controls
and jumped from the crane.
The hook crashed to the ground.

The monster gave an enormous roar
and fell in a tangle on the floor.
His mask dropped off.

"TAT RABBIT!" cried Tig. "You cheater!"

Tat Rabbit giggled.
"I was only teasing," he said, and gave another
roar. "Come and see the treasure. It's . . . it's
splendiferous!"

And it was.